This Walker book belongs to:

Baby Paterson

For Rosemary J. - her book
M.W.

For Ellen
S.F-D.

First published 2002 by Walker Books Ltd
87 Vauxhall Walk, London SE11 5HJ

This edition published 2011

2 4 6 8 10 9 7 5 3

This book has been typeset in Veronan

Printed in China

British Library Cataloguing in Publication Data:
a catalogue record for this book is available from the British Library

ISBN 978-1-4063-3201-8

www.walker.co.uk

Snow Bears

Martin Waddell

illustrated by Sarah Fox-Davies

WALKER BOOKS
AND SUBSIDIARIES
LONDON · BOSTON · SYDNEY · AUCKLAND

Mummy Bear came out to play with her
baby bears. They were all covered with snow.
"You look like snow bears," Mummy Bear said.
"That's what we are," said the three baby bears.
"We are snow bears!"
And that's how their snow bear game began.
"But where are *my* baby bears?" Mummy Bear asked.

"I don't know where we are," said the
   biggest snow bear.
"I haven't seen us," said the
   middle-sized snow bear.
"We aren't here, Mummy Bear," said the
   smallest snow bear.
"Then who can I play with?" sighed Mummy Bear.

"We'll play with you, Mummy Bear," said the snow bears.
"What games will we play?" asked Mummy Bear.
"Let's slide," said the biggest
snow bear.

They slid down the slope and . . .

BOOOOOOOOOOOM!

The smallest snow bear got snow on her nose.
"*My* baby bears would like playing that game,"
Mummy Bear said. "Are you sure you haven't
seen my baby bears?"

"I don't know where
we are," said the
biggest snow bear.

"I haven't seen us,"
said the middle-sized
snow bear.

"We aren't here,
Mummy Bear," said
the smallest snow bear.

"What will we play next?" Mummy Bear asked.
"We snowball you, and
you snowball us,"
said the middle-sized
snow bear.

SPLOT

SPLOT

SPLOT

SPLOT!

The smallest snow bear
couldn't throw very well.
Her paws were as cold
as her nose.

"Three against one isn't fair!" Mummy Bear said.
"I wonder where *my* baby bears can be?"
"I don't know where we are," said the biggest snow bear.
"I haven't seen us," said the middle-sized snow bear.
"We aren't here, Mummy Bear," said the
smallest snow bear.

"It's your turn to pick the next game,"
Mummy Bear said to the smallest snow bear.
"I'm too cold to play games," said the smallest
snow bear. "I want to go home."

"Hot toast by the fire will soon warm you up,"
Mummy Bear said. "My baby bears like hot toast."
"So do we," said the snow bears.

Mummy Bear carried the smallest snow bear
in her arms as they all went back to the
warmth of the house.

DRIP . . .

"Something's happening to us,"
said the biggest snow bear.

DRIP . . . DRIP . . .

"We're starting to drip,"
said the middle-sized
snow bear.

DRIP . . . DRIP . . . DRIP!

"We're melting away," said
the smallest snow bear.

Mummy Bear came back with the toast.
She saw her three baby bears by the
fire where the snow bears had been.
"My baby bears!" Mummy Bear said.
"Yes! It's us!" said the three baby bears.
"But where are the snow bears I left
by the fire?" Mummy Bear asked.

"There weren't any snow bears," said the
biggest baby bear.

"We were playing tricks," said the
middle-sized baby bear.

"It was us all the time, Mummy Bear," said the
smallest baby bear.

"But I made this toast for the snow bears!"
Mummy Bear said.

"We'll eat the toast!" said the three baby bears.

Then they all had hot toast by the fire,
Mummy Bear and her three baby bears.